Copyright © 2000 by Michael Neugebauer Verlag,
an imprint of Nord-Süd Verlag AG, Gossau Zürich, Switzerland.
First published in Switzerland under the title *Danke, reines Wasser!*
English translation copyright © 2002 by North-South Books Inc.

First published in the United States, Great Britain, Canada,
Australia, and New Zealand in 2002 by North-South Books,
an imprint of Nord-Süd Verlag AG, Gossau Zürich, Switzerland.
First paperback edition published in 2003 by North-South Books.

Distributed in the United States by North-South Books Inc., New York.

Library of Congress Cataloging-in-Publication Data
Weninger, Brigitte.
[Danke, reines Wasser! English]
Precious water: a book of thanks / Brigitte Weninger, Anne Möller.
p.   cm.
"A Michael Neugebauer Book." —Cover.
Summary: A young girl celebrates our most precious natural resource,
describes the sources of water and its importance to all living things, and
expresses her gratitude for this gift of nature.
[1. Water—Fiction. 2. Natural resources—Fiction.] I. Möller, Anne, ill. II. Title.
PZ7.W46916 Pr 2002   [E]—dc21   2001044559

A CIP catalogue record for this book is available from The British Library.
ISBN 0-7358-1513-5 (trade edition) 10 9 8 7 6 5 4 3 2 1
ISBN 0-7358-1514-3 (library edition) 10 9 8 7 6 5 4 3 2 1
ISBN 0-7358-1869-X (paperback edition) 10 9 8 7 6 5 4 3 2 1
Printed in Belgium

For more information about our books, and the authors and artists
who create them, visit our web site: www.northsouth.com

A Michael Neugebauer Book
NORTH-SOUTH BOOKS / NEW YORK / LONDON

Look at this glass of water.

Precious Water

A Book of Thanks

Brigitte Weninger

Anne Möller

It is so clear that you can see right through it.

The little drops of water on the glass glitter like jewels, and they are just as precious.

All living things need water.

Without water, the plants would die.

Without water, the animals would die.

Without water, people would die.

The whole world would be dead
if there were no water.

But luckily, we do have water: water that falls from the sky, water in the rivers and lakes and deep beneath the ground.

Ice and snow are frozen water.

And the seas are made of salt water.

I give my plants a little water so they won't wilt.

I give my cat a little water
so she won't be thirsty.

And I drink some water too.
How good it tastes!

I hope we will always have enough water for
the plants and animals and people on earth.
I am so thankful for this precious water.

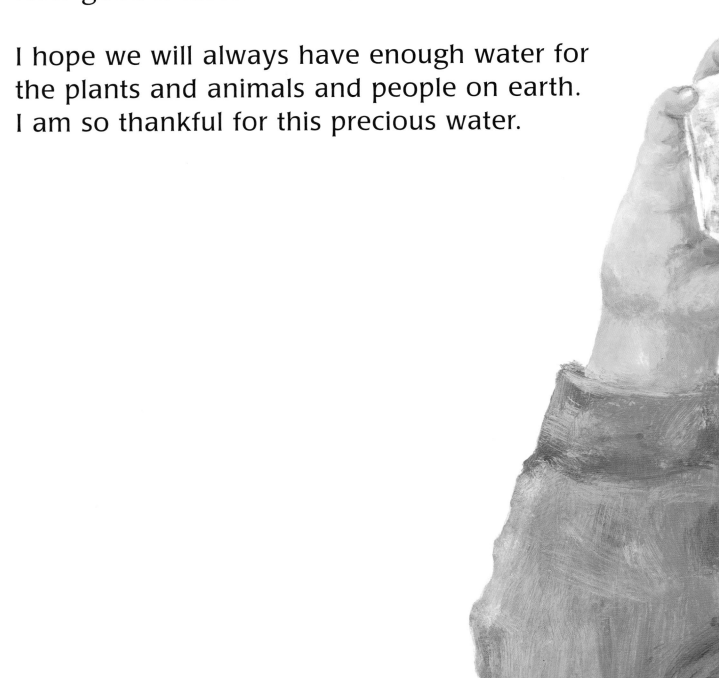